For J, D, H and I

Library and Archives Canada Cataloguing in Publication

Title: Time is a flower / Julie Morstad.
Names: Morstad, Julie, author, illustrator.
Identifiers: Canadiana (print) 20200216341 | Canadiana (ebook) 2020021635X
ISBN 9780735267541 (hardcover) | ISBN 9780735267558 (EPUB)
Classification: LCC PS8626.O777 T56 2021 | DDC jC813/.6—dc23

Published simultaneously in the United States of America by Tundra Books of
Northern New York, an imprint of Penguin Random House Canada Young Readers,
a division of Penguin Random House of Canada Limited

Library of Congress Control Number: 2020936847

Edited by Tara Walker with assistance from Margot Blankier
Designed by John Martz and Julie Morstad
The artwork in this book was made with pencil, markers,
colored inks and pastels, then assembled digitally.
The text was set in Helvetica Now.

Printed in China

www.penguinrandomhouse.ca

1   2   3   4   5   25   24   23   22   21

TIME IS A FLOWER

julie morstad

tundra

Time is the tick tick tock
of the
clock
and
numbers and words
on a calendar.

But what else is time?

Time is a seed.
Sleeping,
waiting
in the dark.

And then . . .

Time is a flower.

Cyclamen,
marigold,
poppy,
violet,
verbena!

With petals so loud and bright,
calling all bees!

Until . . .

The flower droops.

Releasing
its petals,

one
by
one,
or
all at
once.

Time is a tree.

As it grows, so do you.

Who will be taller
in two years?

In ten years?

In fifty years?

Time is a web.

Hard to see,

made slowly,

delicately . . .

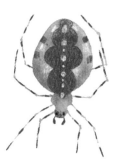

by the careful and elegant spider.

Time is a pebble

that used to be a mountain . . .

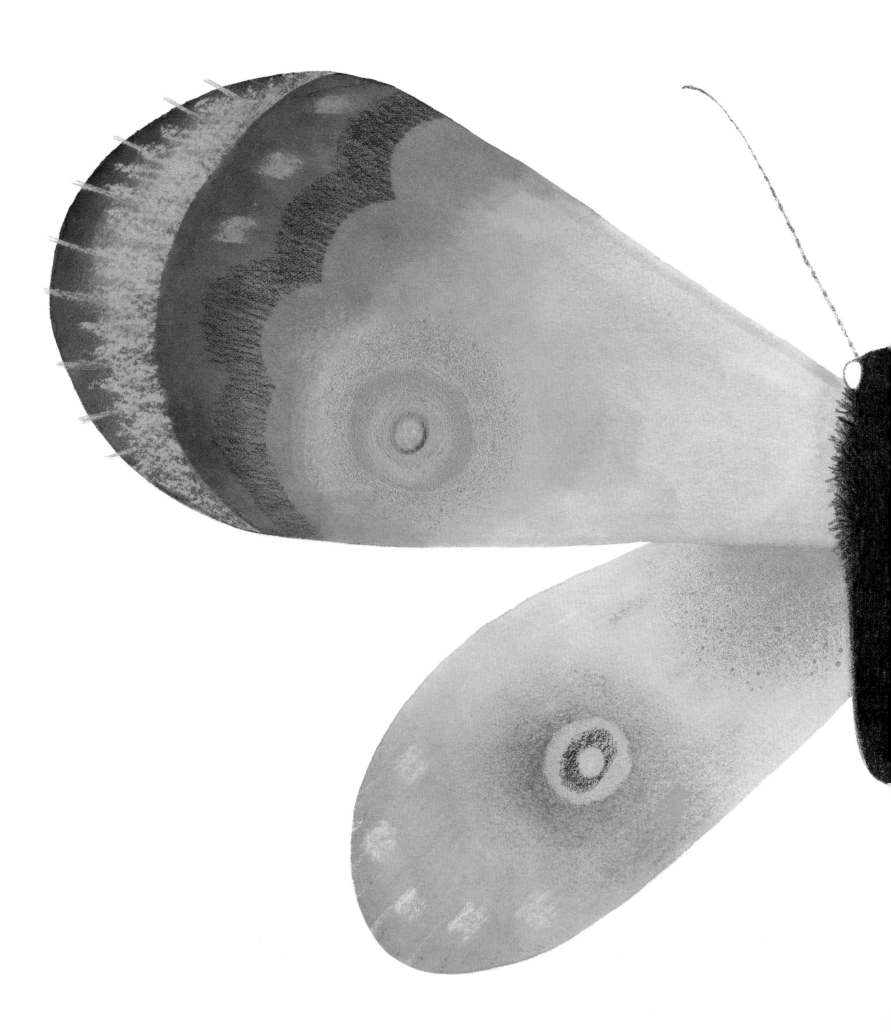

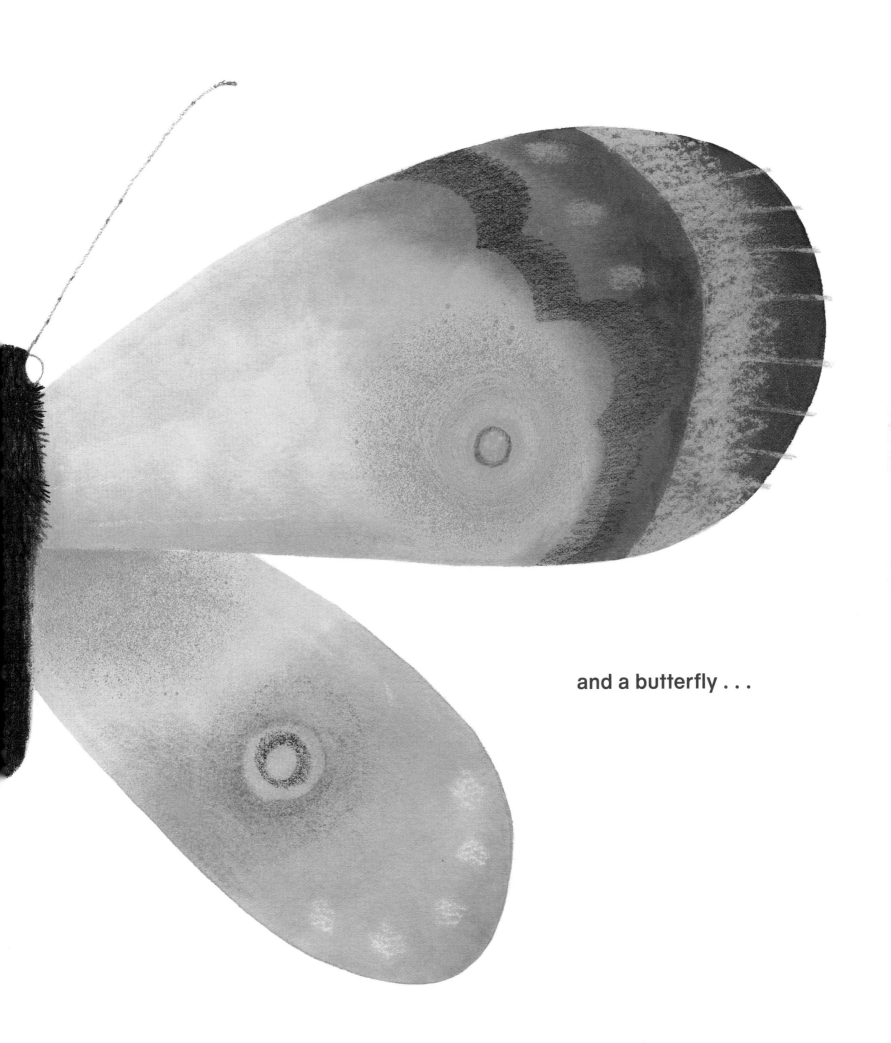

and a butterfly . . .

that used to be a caterpillar.

Time is a sunset.

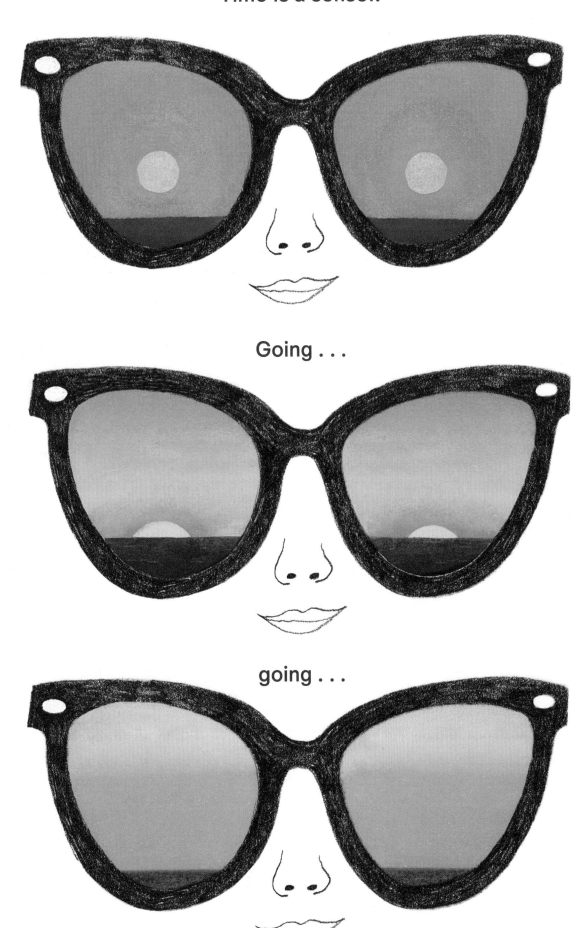

Going . . .

going . . .

gone.

Time is night for someone.

And day for someone else.

Time is a sunbeam,
changing
the shadows
and shapes
of everything.

The sleeping cat
knows this.

Time is a memory
captured long ago,
in a tiny part of a second.

Now,
of all the seconds
that ever happened,
this one is forever.

And maybe it seems
like yesterday.

Time is your
hair growing

long,
long,
longer . . .

Then quick!

That time disappears in a SNIP!

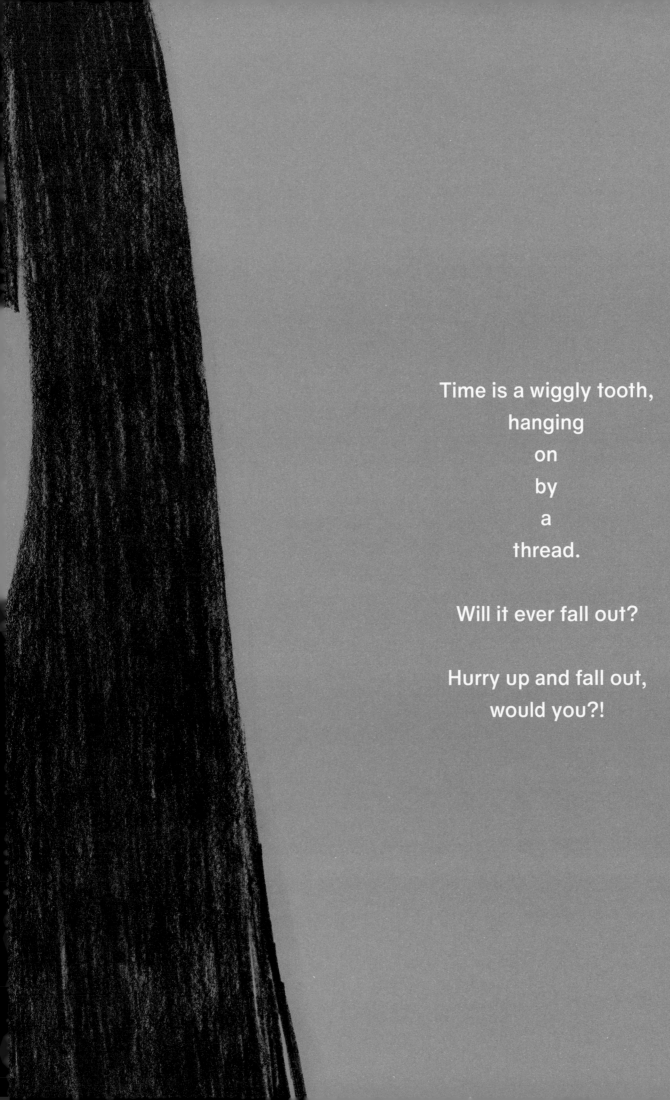

Time is a wiggly tooth,
hanging
on
by
a
thread.

Will it ever fall out?

Hurry up and fall out,
would you?!

Time is a face whose lines and shapes

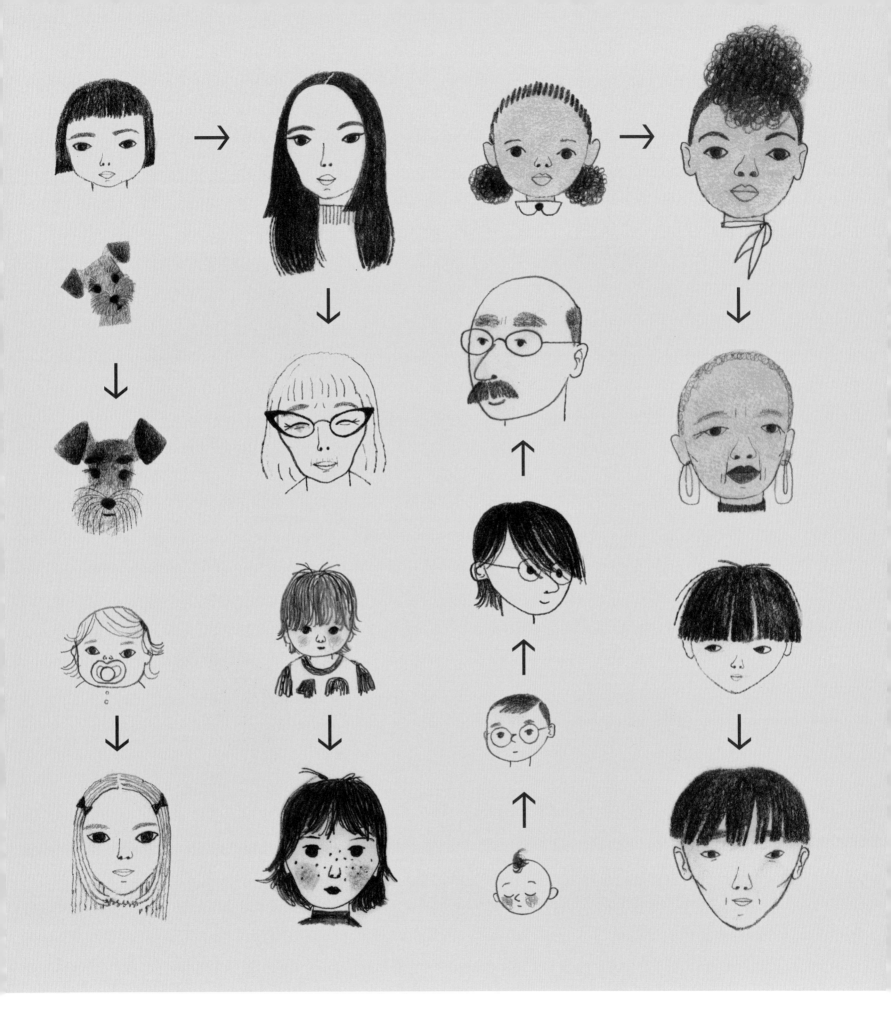

change little by little, year by year.

Time can move slowly,

counting

down

the minutes

until . . .

SCHOOL'S OUT!

Or time can move fast!

Like the wave that
just caught your
best sandcastle.

Time is a song.

Dancing you quick!

Hands clapping,
heels clicking.

Or pulling you,

long and stretching,

slow and low,
to the sound of a cello.

Time is a batch of bread,

mixing

rising

punching

rising again . . .

baking . . .

And then —

the
loafy
squish!

Delicious!

Time is
staying there
to think about what you did.

Maybe you didn't
mean to?

Time is a story, or three.

Is time a line?

16 17 18 19 20 21 22

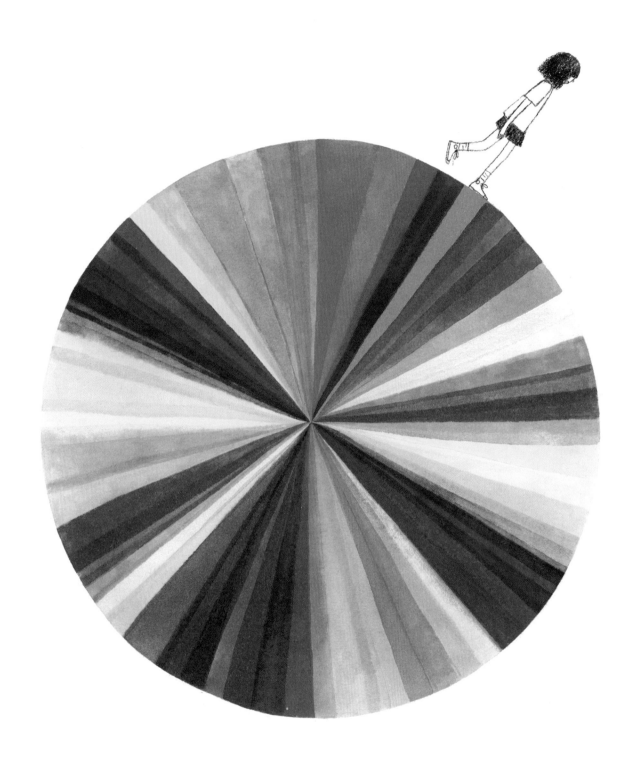

Or maybe a circle?

I don't know,
but
it's time for dinner.